Nightmare on Hannah Street

Adapted by Laurie McElroy

Based on the series created by Michael Poryes and Rich Correll & Barry O'Brien

Part One is based on the episode, "Torn Between Two Hannahs," Story by Valerie Ahern & Christian McLaughlin
Teleplay by Todd J. Greenwald

Part Two is based on the episode, "Grandma Don't Let Your Babies Grow Up To Play Favourites,"
Written by Douglas Lieblein

Bath · New York · Singapore · Hong Kong · Cologne · Delhi · Melbourne

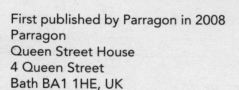

First published by Parragon in 2008
Parragon
Queen Street House
4 Queen Street
Bath BA1 1HE, UK

ISBN 978-1-4075-4648-3
Printed in UK

PART ONE

Chapter One

Miley Stewart, along with her best friends, Lilly Truscott and Oliver Oken, listened to her father play a new song. Mr Stewart strummed his guitar and then launched into the lyrics. Miley joined in with her strong, clear voice, reading the lyrics her father had written.

When the song was over, Lilly and Oliver applauded wildly. Not only was it a terrific song, it was perfect for Hannah Montana.

Miley's best friends were the only two people in the world outside of her family who knew her secret.

When it came to secrets, this was a big one.

Miley Stewart led a double life. Most days, she was just a regular girl in senior school. But at night, she became pop-music sensation Hannah Montana. Hannah was the queen of the teen music world.

Miley loved being Hannah on-stage, but offstage she was happy to take off her blonde Hannah wig and pop star clothes and go back to being Miley Stewart. She wanted people to like her for who she was and not because she was famous. That meant living like a normal girl and keeping her double life a secret.

Miley gave her father a high five. She knew this song would make Hannah more

popular than ever. "Dad, that's awesome. That is the best song you've ever written, I can't wait to record it."

Then Miley remembered the last time her father wrote her a really great song. The song was the best – but the news that came along with it was the worst. "What's the bad news?" she asked.

"Bad news?" Lilly asked, confused. "What are you talking about? It's a great song."

"Thank you, Lilly," Mr Stewart said. He turned to Miley. "I've always liked her," he said, nodding in Lilly's direction.

"Don't change the subject," Miley said seriously.

Mr Stewart *did* have some news, but he wasn't telling – yet. Lilly and Oliver looked even more confused.

"Every time he has bad news he tries to soften it with a great song," Miley explained

5

to her friends. She had a list of top-ten songs and the bad news that went along with them, and she could tell the list was about to get longer. She laid some of them out for Lilly and Oliver.

"'Best of Both Worlds' – I had to get braces. 'This Is the Life' – Jackson decided not to go to sleepaway camp. 'Pumpin' Up the Party' – my goldfish died."

Miley's goldfish triggered one of Oliver's memories. "When my goldfish died, my mum flushed it down the toilet," he said. "I'll never forget her comforting words – 'Get over it, Oliver, it's a stinking fish.'"

Lilly nodded knowingly. "That explains so much."

But Miley didn't want to hear about Oliver's fish. "Come on, Dad, just tell me. Trust me, I can handle it."

Mr Stewart took a breath before speaking. "Your cousin Luann is coming to visit," he said quickly. Then he turned to Lilly and Oliver and tried to change the subject. "Who wants pie?"

Luann? Miley stared at her father, completely stunned. That was the worst news ever. When she became Hannah Montana, Miley and her father and brother, Jackson, had left Tennessee and moved to California.

Miley loved her new friends and their beach house in Malibu, but sometimes she missed everyone in the big extended family they had left back home. Everyone except Luann. The name Luann was so horrifying to her that Miley couldn't speak, couldn't move, couldn't scream.

"Miley?" Lilly asked

"Miley?" Mr Stewart repeated, waving a hand in front of her face.

Miley didn't even blink. She was totally

frozen.

Oliver didn't notice. "What kind of pie?" he asked, jumping to his feet and running to the kitchen.

"C'mon, Mile," Mr Stewart said. "Don't forget that wonderful, wonderful song that I just wrote for you, that you love so much." He picked up his guitar again and sang as he played.

Miley put her hand on the guitar strings, stopping him. She didn't want to hear the song right now – not when her father had just spat out the terrible news. "When does her broomstick land?" she asked through clenched teeth.

"Come on there, Mile. Don't start this again," Mr Stewart said, heading towards the kitchen. "She's a good kid. Let's not forget who pulled you out of that well when you were just six."

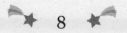

"Let's not forget who pushed me in," Miley said, following him.

"Hey, that was an accident. Sometimes kids do stuff without thinking," Mr Stewart said.

Miley shook her head. Luann had their parents totally fooled, but Miley knew the truth. Luann was bad news – really bad news.

Oliver had cut himself a huge slice of cherry pie and was eating it at the kitchen table. A fly buzzed around his head and landed on his slice. He slammed his hand down, missing the fly, but knocking his plate into his lap and getting pie all over himself. "Stupid fly," Oliver said, spreading cherry filling across his T-shirt.

Miley and Lilly looked on in disbelief as he picked up his fork and started eating again. But Mr Stewart used Oliver's mess to make his point about accidents.

"I didn't plan that," he said. "But there you go."

"I can't believe this," Miley said. "Halloween is two days away and you want me to share my bathroom with the Princess of Darkness? If she's coming, I'm sleeping at Lilly's." Miley turned on her heel and stormed off in the direction of the front door.

"Oh, come on, Mile," her father said, trying to reason with her. "You guys have both grown up. She's grown up. You've grown up. You're a lot alike."

Alike? Miley turned to her father, totally outraged. "How can you say that? I'm nothing like that horrible, ugly witch."

The doorbell rang. Miley opened the front door and found herself face-to-face with her hated cousin. Luann was in all her Tennessee finery – pigtails, a bright red shirt that looked like an overgrown bandanna and a straw cowboy hat. People had been telling both girls for years that they looked alike, but Miley didn't see it. She glared at her cousin.

Luann blinked behind her glasses and flashed Miley a big grin. "Howdy, cuz!" she said.

Lightning flashed, followed by a crash of thunder. Evil is in the air, Miley thought.

Lilly's jaw dropped, and she was too stunned to close it again. Oliver's eyes popped. Luann and Miley looked like twins!

Luann ignored everyone's shock and confusion. "Eeeee doggies!" she declared. "This is one humdinger of a shack!"

Chapter Two

Miley was in the kitchen alone eating pie, but she kept a close eye on Luann. Jackson had come bounding down the stairs when he heard Luann's Tennessee drawl. Now everyone was crowded around her in the living room like she was visiting royalty or something, Miley thought.

Luann was pretending that she was happy to see everyone, but Miley was convinced that only meant something awful was about to happen – to Miley.

She watched Luann pull a tin out of her suitcase and hand it to Mr Stewart.

"Uncle Robby," she drawled with a smile. "Daddy said that these were your favourite Halloween cookies. I made them myself."

Mr Stewart opened the tin and everyone reached in for a cookie.

"Pecan crunchies! Sweet, nutty niblets," Mr Stewart said, digging in.

Miley rolled her eyes. They were all way too excited about a few cookies.

"Mmm," Jackson said, letting the cookie melt on his tongue. "You churned your own butter, didn't you?"

"Is there any other way?" Luann asked.

Lilly carried her cookie into the kitchen and sat next to Miley.

"Whatever you do, don't eat that," Miley whispered.

"Why not?" Lilly asked.

"Because it was made by the devil's little helper," Miley said with a grim expression.

"You're being ridiculous," Lilly said. She took a bite of her cookie and then clutched her throat dramatically before starting to gag. Lilly spat out her bite, threw the cookie in the air and toppled off her chair onto the floor.

"Lilly!" Miley said, totally irritated.

"Oh, please," Lilly said, dropping the act. "Next you'll be saying . . ." she leaned in and whispered in a spooky voice, ". . . she sees dead people."

Miley ignored her and focused on what was going on in the living room. Luann was sucking up, as usual.

"You know," Oliver was saying, "it's amazing how much you and Miley look alike."

Luann nodded. "Always have. When we were young 'uns, you know, before she was Hanner Montanner, she was in the Little Miss Tater pageant, but I had to take her place just before the talent part when she got all nervous and barfy."

Miley fumed in the kitchen. "I wasn't nervous," she told Lilly. "She slipped me some bad catfish. She's always been jealous of me because I can sing and she can't."

"So what'd she do for talent?" Lilly asked.

Oliver must have asked Luann the same question, because a few seconds later they heard Luann's "talent" from across the room.

"Suuuuuu-ey!" Luann called.

"Pig calls," Miley said. She'd never forget it. For weeks afterwards all the boys in her class followed her around making pig-calling noises. It was totally humiliating, and Luann just smiled and laughed.

"Su-su-su-suuuuuu-ey!" Luann called again.

Mr Stewart turned to Jackson. "Man, I miss Tennessee," he said.

Jackson nodded in agreement.

Oliver was totally mesmerized. He listed Luann's talents for Mr Stewart. "Boy, she cooks, she calls pigs." Then he turned to Luann. "Where have you been all my life?" he asked, leaning over the sofa.

"Oh, you!" Luann gave Oliver what looked like a playful slap on the shoulder, but she didn't know her own strength.

Oliver hit the floor with a loud thud.

"Momma warned me about you handsome Californy fellers," Luann said with a grin.

Oliver got to his feet and tried to laugh

it off. "Oh, you . . ." he needed a snappy comeback, but he didn't have one. He edged away from Luann in case she decided to hit him again. He gave Luann a playful slap back. "Too," he said weakly.

Miley watched it all from the kitchen, rolling her eyes.

"Didn't you say you named your pet pig Luann?" Lilly asked.

"Yep," Miley said.

They watched Luann laughing with Mr Stewart in the living room. Suddenly, she let out a giant snort, then laughed and snorted some more.

"And now you know why," Miley said.

Later that day, Mr Stewart carried a box into the living room and set it down on the coffee table. Jackson was rummaging through another box and pulled out an old plastic Dracula decoration with a comical-looking owl sitting on his shoulder. It was about as scary as a Saturday morning cartoon.

"This is pathetic," Jackson said. "Every year we put up the same stupid decorations and all my friends laugh at us."

"I don't know. I think these are pretty gruesome." Mr Stewart pulled a giant, furry spider out of his box and held it over Jackson's head. "Look out, a spider," he yelled.

Jackson didn't flinch, so Mr Stewart kept trying. "It's in your hair! It's crawling in your hair. It's on your shoulder!" Then he gave up. "Boo," he said quietly.

Jackson shook his head. The lame spider totally proved his point. "Pathetic," he said. "Can we get something halfway decent this year? Our Christmas decorations are scarier than this."

Mr Stewart shook his head. He liked the old decorations. He liked Dracula. He liked the furry spider. He liked tradition. And their Christmas decorations were NOT scary. "Hey, just because one of Santa's eyes fell out doesn't make him any less jolly," he said defensively.

There was a knock on the door and Mr Stewart was happy to have a reason to change the subject. "This stuff scares six-year-olds," he said over his shoulder. "It's not like we're gonna find something that scares us."

Mr Stewart opened the door and pretended to scream when he found his neighbour Mr Dontzig standing there in his usual outfit – swimming trunks and a robe tied over his big, round stomach. Had today's robe been orange, he would have looked like a giant pumpkin. But it was black, with pictures of pumpkins, spiders' webs and bats all over it.

"Stewart!" Mr Dontzig snapped. "Someone shoved your magazines in my post box."

"I'm guessing that would be the postman," Mr Stewart answered. He didn't point out that the magazines had obviously been read before being returned.

Mr Dontzig looked over Mr Stewart's shoulder. "What's with the Halloween decorations?" he sneered. "Or should I say Halloweenie decorations?" He laughed at his own joke.

Mr Stewart simply looked at him.

"Your winking Santa was scarier than this," Mr Dontzig said, imitating the one-eyed decoration. "You know, I was hoping this year you'd be a little competition for me. But I was wrong."

Jackson stood at his father's side, glaring at Mr Dontzig. "Dad, are you just gonna let him get away with that?"

"Relax, son," Mr Stewart answered calmly. "It's a holiday. We're not gonna get sucked into his little game."

"Said the loser," Mr Dontzig taunted.

Mr Stewart shook his head. "Don't go challenging me, Dontzig," he warned.

"Ooooh, I'm shaking," Mr Dontzig answered, pretending to quiver all over.

"Well, take it outside," Mr Stewart joked. "I don't have earthquake insurance." He nudged Jackson.

Jackson crossed his arms with a grin and nodded. That's one for Dad, he thought.

Mr Dontzig sneered again. "Save the jokes, *Goldilocks*."

Mr Stewart bristled. Goldilocks?

"You'll need a sense of humour when

kids see how unscary your house is and start pelting it with eggs," Mr Dontzig warned. "Which would be an improvement on this paint job." He cackled and flicked a paint chip off the door before imitating the one-eyed Santa again.

Mr Stewart watched his neighbour head back to his own house through narrowed eyes. "That's it. He crossed the line. He insulted my hair," Mr Stewart said. "Now get in the car. We're about to put the 'boo' in Malibu."

Jackson pumped his fist in the air. "Yes!"

"It's gonna be a hair-raising experience," his father said as he grabbed the car keys. No one made fun of his hair and got away with it!

Chapter Three

Miley and Lilly hung out at Rico's Surf Shop on the beach watching Luann show a little girl how to twirl a lasso.

"I don't know why you're making such a big deal about your cousin," Lilly said, noticing how much fun the little girl was having. "Luann seems really nice."

Miley smiled a big, fake smile and pretended to be enthusiastic. "Yeah, and a Venus flytrap seems like a pretty plant," she said. Then she got serious. "Until it throws you down a well. Trust me, underneath those little piggy tails. . ." Miley stopped to demonstrate by holding her index fingers behind of her head and bending them to make devil's horns. ". . . are little tiny horns."

Lilly just didn't get it. Luann hadn't done anything but try to be nice to Miley. So why was Miley so dead set against being friends with her cousin? "Not to sound like your Dad, but . . ." Lilly deepened her voice and practised her Mr Stewart impersonation. "Maybe you should give her a chance, bud," she drawled. "Now if you'll excuse me, I hear the ice cream truck a-ringin' and I want me a Fudgybuddy."

Miley laughed. Lilly sounded just like Mr Stewart. "Okay, that was creepy good," she said.

"Thanks," Lilly said. But clearly Miley still wasn't willing to hang out with Luann, so she tried again in her own voice. "Would it kill you to open up a little and at least try to be friends with her?" Lilly asked. "Traci's having that big Halloween party tomorrow night. Why don't we take her with us?"

Miley looked at her friend as if she were totally crazy. Traci's father was a big record company executive. Traci was a friend of Hannah Montana's, not Miley Stewart's, and didn't know anything about Miley and her secret double life. Even Lilly always donned a purple wig and pretended to be Lola Luftnagle, Hannah Montana's best friend, when Traci was around.

There was no way Miley wanted Luann anywhere near Traci and her celebrity world. She had worked too hard to keep

Miley and Hannah's worlds apart. "No way!" she said. "I'm not letting that pig-calling, butter-churning, evil-doing hay-seed anywhere near the Hannah world."

Lilly shook her head. "Would you stop calling her names?" She would have said more – she might even have used her Mr Stewart voice again – but Luann walked up to them at that moment and handed Miley a beautiful conch shell.

"Well howdy, cuz. I found you this purty shell over by the tide pools."

"Yeah, pretty," Miley said suspiciously. She dropped the shell on the Surf Shop's counter. "A pretty good place to hide a hermit crab!" She grabbed a napkin holder and smashed the near-perfect shell into little tiny pieces.

"What are you doing?" Luann asked. She looked totally hurt and confused.

"Ruining your little plan to poison me and throw me down a well again," Miley answered. She eyed the shell pieces, looking for evidence of Luann's wicked plot.

"Miley, stop," Lilly said. "There's nothing in there."

Luann's eyes filled with tears. "I was just trying to be nice to y'all." She ran off, choking back tears.

But Miley wasn't swayed by those phony tears. "See how clever she is?" she asked Lilly. "She tricked me into accusing her of something she hadn't done so I'd look stupid."

"Well, it worked. You look stupid," Lilly said.

"I told you." Miley rubbed her hands together like a mad scientist. "She's an evil genius."

Lilly shook her head and walked off, leaving Miley alone.

Jackson had finished going through all the scary Halloween decorations he and his father had picked out. He wore a plastic "bloody" machete on his head. It looked like it had sliced through his skull.

He peeked out of the door, watching for Miley. As soon as he spotted her he sat on the floor, holding his head at a strange angle. He stared straight ahead without blinking, so she would think he was dead.

"Hey, Jackson," Miley said, breezing by him totally unfazed. Jackson had been trying to gross her out for years. A machete and fake Halloween blood weren't going to make her scream.

"Aw, man. It's not scary enough," Jackson said, getting to his feet. "It needs something. But what?" He tapped the axe handle. Think. Think, he told himself.

Miley ignored him. She flopped on the couch. She needed to think about this whole Luann situation. Was it possible that her cousin had changed? Was Lilly right? Was Miley being too hard on Luann?

"So, Mile, what happened at the beach with you and Luann?" her father asked, coming downstairs. "She's up in the guest room awfully upset."

Miley cringed. "It could have something to do with the fact that I accused her of trying to kill me."

Mr Stewart nodded. "Yep. That has been known to offend a person."

"You really think I'm being unfair?" Miley asked.

"Yeah, I do, bud," Mr Stewart said. "But I also know you're awfully good at fixing things when you put your mind to it."

Miley wasn't totally convinced that Luann wasn't evil, but she hated the fact that all of a sudden *she* was the one who looked like the bad guy. "Okay, fine," she said with a big sigh. "I'll go and talk to her."

"That's my girl," her father said.

She started upstairs, then stopped and turned with a warning. "If I'm not down in ten minutes, check all the local wells."

Miley reluctantly knocked on the door to the guest room. "Luann, you okay?"

"Yep," Luann called from the other side of the door. "Just packing up my bags and working on a plan for world domination," she drawled sarcastically.

Luann obviously wasn't going to open the door, so Miley talked through it. It was hard to actually spit out the words. "Look

". . . maybe . . . possibly . . . it's conceivable that I haven't treated you completely fairly," Miley said. She clenched her teeth and lowered her voice for the next part. "And I wanted to say I'm sorry."

Luann looked up from her packing in surprise. Was Miley actually apologizing? "Really?" she asked.

Miley answered in a small voice. "Yeah."

Luann opened the door. Maybe it was time she confessed, too. "The truth is, I always was a little jealous," she admitted.

"Well, I think it's time that we took the past and buried it," Miley said.

"Yeah," Luann agreed. "Kinda like we used to do with Aunt Pearl's roadkill ravioli."

Miley shuddered, remembering just how awful that roadkill ravioli tasted. "There was always gravel in mine," she laughed.

"Yeah, she said it gave it that special crunch," Luann said.

Miley couldn't believe it. There was something she and Luann actually agreed on. Maybe her father and Lilly were right. She hadn't really given Luann a chance. Miley decided that since she had come this far, it was time to take another step.

"Well, if you still want to stay, there's a really great Hollywood Halloween party that I'd love to take you to," Miley said.

Luann's eyes filled with tears again, but these were happy ones. "You really want me to come with you-ins?" she asked.

Miley nodded. "I really want you to come with . . ." she had to stop and think about the right word . . . "me-ins," she said finally.

"I'm touched." Luann put her hand over

her heart. She didn't have to say yes. Her smile said it for her.

The next night, Lilly arrived at the same time as the limo that was going to take the girls to Traci's Halloween party. She and Miley had decided to go to the party dressed as Hannah Montana and Lola. There was no need for other costumes. All Lilly had to do was put on her purple wig, lots of make-up and funky Lola clothes.

She ran up the stairs and into Miley's bedroom. She didn't see Miley, so she opened the secret door in the back of Miley's wardrobe that led to the hidden Hannah Montana dressing room. It was about ten times bigger than Miley's regular wardrobe.

"Hey, the limo's here to take us to Traci's party. You ready?" Lilly asked.

Miley was putting the finishing touches to her Hannah look, which included a long blonde wig, skinny jeans and a glittery Hannah top. "Oh, yeah, let's do this," she answered.

"Where's Luann?" Lilly asked, looking around.

"Oh, um, she can't go," Miley said. "She was at the beach boogie-boarding all day and got really bad sunburn."

"Oooh, I hate that," Lilly said sympathetically. "But at least the two of you are friends now."

"Yep, the best of pals," Miley said, pushing Lilly towards the door. "Let's go."

They were almost out the door when Miley realized she was missing something. "I forgot my bag," she said. "I'll meet you in the limo, okay?"

"Okay," Lilly answered.

Miley closed the door behind Lilly and pushed the button on the wall that made the clothes in her wardrobe turn like a carousel.

She threw back her head and let out an evil Luann cackle when the real Miley, wearing the exact same outfit as the fake Miley, spun into view. Luann had hogtied Miley just like a calf in a rodeo. There was a purple feather boa wrapped around Miley's head and tied in a bow.

Miley's eyes got wide when she spotted Luann, dressed as Hannah. Luann's plan became clear – she was going to go to the party in Miley's place.

Suddenly the fake Miley lost her California accent and started talking with her Tennessee drawl again. "Miley, Miley, Miley," Luann said. "I can't believe you didn't see this a-comin'. Maybe if you wouldn't have wasted your time in singing classes and went to rodeo camp with the rest of us, you wouldn't be stuck in this sitchiation."

Miley wanted to tell her backstabbing cousin exactly what she thought of her, but the boa in her mouth made it impossible. She tried to kick her feet, but Luann had tied the knots so tight that she could hardly move.

"What's that, girl?" Luann asked, clearly enjoying every minute of Miley's discomfort. "You want Hannah to perform at the party? Good idea."

Luann struck a pose and burst into song.

Even with rage pounding in her ears, Miley could hear how ghastly and off-key Luann's voice was.

"Horrible, ain't it?" Luann asked with a

wicked grin. "Wait until your 'fans' hear that. That'll do wonders for your career." Luann chuckled and slung her bag over her shoulder. "Happy Halloween, cuz!" she yelled and then burst into a chilling, cackling laugh.

All Miley could do was watch her leave. She tried to spit the boa out of her mouth. Feathers flew in the air around her, but she still couldn't speak.

Chapter Four

Jackson and Mr Stewart worked all day to turn their front porch into a haunted Halloween mansion. Spiders' webs hung from the walls and the banisters. The front door had been replaced with old wooden boards that made it look like a coffin, and an eerie, ghostly laugh came from the stereo speakers.

Mr Stewart was dressed as a scarecrow with a pumpkin head. He sat in a chair, ready to greet the trick-or-treaters. A group of little kids dressed as fire fighters, cowgirls, tramps and bumblebees trotted up the path and rang the doorbell.

"Trick or treat!" they called.

Jackson popped out of the coffin/door dressed in an unravelling mummy costume. At the same time, Mr Stewart got to his feet and yelled, "Boo!"

The kids screamed and started to run.

Mr Stewart pulled off his pumpkin head and called after them. "Wait, kids. You forgot your candy."

"Yes!" Jackson said, taking off his zombie mask. "There is no way Dontzig's house is scarier than ours."

Mr Stewart and Jackson high fived each other just as the kids came back up the path. Some of them were crying and this time their parents were with them.

"What is wrong with you?" asked one mother.

"You're supposed to hand out candy, not traumatize my kid!" yelled another.

The rest of the parents nodded in agreement, while their children hid behind them.

"I'm sorry," Mr Stewart said. "You don't understand. See, we're just trying to be as scary as the guy next door."

"You mean Mr Happy Pumpkin Man?" asked the first mother.

"Who?" Jackson asked.

"Hey, hey kids!" Mr Dontzig said, running through a gap in the hedge with a huge smile on his face. He was wearing a giant pumpkin costume. The pumpkin's smile was just as big as Mr Dontzig's. "Oh, is mean old Mr Stewart scaring you?" he asked.

The kids ran to the happy pumpkin and hid behind him.

Mr Stewart's jaw dropped. "I don't believe this," he said. Hadn't Mr Dontzig challenged him to have a spooky, scary Halloween house?

"Why would somebody want to scare little children?" Mr Dontzig asked the parents. Then he turned to Mr Stewart and wagged a finger at him. "It's *sick*."

The parents clearly agreed.

"I'm not surprised," one of the mothers said. "At Christmas, they had a one-eyed Santa."

"It's true. I've seen it," another mother added.

"But this is Halloween," Jackson said, desperately trying to save the situation. "And you're in Mali-boo." As he said the words, he pulled the zombie mask in front of his face.

The kids started screaming again and hugged Mr Dontzig even tighter.

"C'mon, kids," Mr Dontzig said triumphantly. "Let's all go back to my house and everyone can have another ride on the pony." He jumped up and down and led the kids in a cheer, followed by a song.

"He's Mr Happy Pumpkin Man, giving out candy like no one can," they sang as they filed through the gap in the hedge, followed by their parents.

Mr Dontzig turned to his neighbours. "Well, Stewarts, you win," he said with a big smile. "You're the scariest. And everyone in the neighbourhood hates you."

Mr Stewart stared at him through narrowed eyes as the truth dawned on him. His neighbour had set them up for this. It was part of a grand plan to make the whole neighbourhood hate the Stewarts.

"Gotcha!" Mr Dontzig shouted as he followed the kids into his own front garden, singing. *"He's Mr Happy Pumpkin Man, giving out candy like no one can."*

"Wait up, kids!" Mr Stewart called. "I'm sorry."

"Hey, hey," Jackson said. "Don't forget your candy."

The two of them ran off after Mr Dontzig.

One of the mothers spotted them. "Get away from our children," she yelled.

"I've got pepper spray!" another added.

Jackson and Mr Stewart were still in Mr Dontzig's garden trying to explain, when Miley finally freed herself and ran out onto the front porch.

"Dad? Jackson?" she called. Miley barely noticed the scary decorations. She had to get to that party before Luann ruined Hannah Montana's reputation. But her father and Jackson were nowhere to be seen and she didn't have time to waste. She grabbed her mobile phone – at least Luann hadn't got her hands on that – and punched in Oliver's number.

"Oliver, I need your mum to drive me to a Halloween party *now*," she said when he answered. She rolled her eyes when she heard his response. "Yes, you can come."

The ride seemed to take forever, but Miley and Oliver finally walked up to the big party tent where Traci was throwing her Halloween bash. A creepy fog covered the path. Stone goblins holding torches in their mouths lit the way.

"I can't believe Luann would tie you up and try to ruin your life," Oliver said. "You know, this is going to make my date with her tomorrow a little awkward."

Miley glared at him. Her life was about

to be ruined and Oliver was thinking about a date? She pulled Oliver's mask and let it snap back onto his face.

"What are you going to do when you see her?" Oliver asked.

"I'm going to rip her wig off and punch her in the nose," Miley said. "Just help me find her. It's not going to be that hard, she'll be the only one in there that looks exactly like me."

Miley opened the tent flaps. Her jaw dropped when she realized she was looking into a tent full of girls wearing Hannah Montana costumes. A huge banner in the back of the room read HAPPY HANNAHWEEN.

"Oh, boy," she said, letting the tent close again. She turned to Oliver. "This is going to be a little harder than I thought."

Chapter Five

Lilly's eyes widened in disbelief, as Luann, who Lilly still thought was Miley, filled her bag with candy from the food table. She was acting totally uncool. Hannah Montana was on the A-list, and yet she was acting like someone who'd never been to a Hollywood party before.

"Ooh-wee, these gummy ghouls are better than Pappy's mountain taffy!"

"Man, you've been hanging around your

cousin so much, you're starting to talk like her," Lilly said. She pulled the candy bowl out of Miley's hands. "And stop loading up on the candy. People are watching."

"Of course they are," Luann said gleefully. "I'm a ceeee-lebrity." She grabbed the bowl back and dumped the rest of the gummy ghouls into her bag.

Traci walked over wearing a long, blonde Hannah wig and tried to give Hannah Montana the air kisses that were so prevalent in Hollywood.

Lilly watched Miley pull back as if she didn't know what was happening.

"Hannah," Traci said in her nasally, high voice. "You've been here an hour and you haven't said a word about my little Hannahween surprise."

"Oh," Luann said. "You mean everyone dressed like me?"

Traci nodded.

"Yeah, it's about as stupid as a vegetarian havin' breakfast at the Beef 'n' Waffle," Luann said. Then she turned her back on Traci and started emptying another candy bowl into her bag.

"What are you talking about?" With a horrified expression, Traci watched Miley shovel the candy into her bag.

"I'm talking about stupid," Luann said. "Just like your stupid little voice. What's the matter, you got a candy corn stuck up in your nozzle?"

Traci's face went from confused to angry and insulted in seconds. "I have a deviated septum, and I admit it." She snapped her fingers in Luann's face and turned her back on her before storming off.

"What's wrong with you?" Lilly asked. "You've been acting weird since we got here. It's like you want the whole party to hate you." Suddenly the truth dawned on her. Lilly's eyes popped. "Omigosh," she gasped. "You're Luann."

"Well, it took you long enough, Lulu," Luann said, dropping any attempt to speak in Miley's accent.

Lilly glared at her. "It's Lola."

"Lilly, Lola, Lulu, you might as well go by Purple Head," Luann said, tugging on Lilly's bright lavender wig. "What do you use for conditioner? Grape jelly?" she taunted.

Then she spotted a waiter. "Hey, waiter! Fetch me some peanut butter. I'd like to make me a sammich," she said in a laugh that ended in a snort.

"I've got to get you out of here before you blow Miley's secret," Lilly said in a whisper.

Luann's face lit up. "Well, shut my mouth. I wasn't even thinking about pulling this wig off till you done brought it up," she said. "That'd really fix her wagon." She patted Lilly's head. "Good job, gumdrop."

Lilly tried to stop her, but Luann darted out of her grasp and into the crowd. Not only was Luann going to blow Miley's secret, Lilly had given her the idea!

The real Miley and Oliver were scanning the crowd of Hannahs looking for Luann.

"I had a dream like this once," Oliver said. "Except it was a room full of Jessica Simpsons and I had more than one chest hair."

"Focus," Miley said. "We have to find the *real* fake Hannah."

Lilly rushed up, pushed Oliver out of the way, and grabbed Miley. "Gotcha! I am not going to let you ruin my best friend's life."

"I am your best friend," Miley said.

"You can't fool me with that fake accent," Lilly answered.

"I am Miley," she insisted. "I have to go and find Luann!"

Miley tried to move away, but Lilly was determined to hold onto her. She grabbed Miley's nose.

"You're not going anywhere without your nose."

Oliver got to his feet and stood behind Miley. "Lilly, she's telling the truth."

"Oliver?" Lilly said, suddenly realizing who she had pushed out of her way a minute ago. Was Oliver in on Luann's evil plot? "What are you doing here?" she asked.

Miley tried to explain, even though Lilly still had her nose pinched between her fingers. "I needed his mum to drive me here, after you and Luann rode off in my limo!" she said, sounding like she had the worst cold in the world.

"Miley?" Lilly asked, looking into her best friend's eyes.

"Ya think?" Miley said, still sounding all stuffed up.

"Sorry." Lilly let go of Miley's nose. "We have to find her quick. She's about to rip off her wig and blow your secret."

"She wouldn't!" Miley said.

"She would. And she thought of it all herself . . ." Lilly said, remembering that she had given Luann the idea for her evil plan. "Remember, no matter what she says, she's evil."

The three friends looked at each other in silent agreement and then split up looking for Luann.

"Looking for Hannah," Lilly said to herself passing a look-alike. "Not you," she said.

Oliver turned a girl around who was roughly Miley's height. "Not you," he said when he got a look at her face. "But, hi," he added with a smile when he saw how pretty she was.

A Hannah twirled around in front of Miley. She was old enough to be Miley's grandmother. "Not you, but girl aren't you styling!" Miley said.

She might have said more, but just then Luann took the stage at the back of the tent. Miley shuddered when she noticed Luann holding a microphone. Was she going to do something that would end Hannah Montana's career, or would she settle for ruining Miley's normal life?

"Hey, folks, it's me, the real Hannah Montana!" Luann said. "I've got a little announcement for y'all, so you might want to get out your fancy Hollywood phone cameras for this one."

Lilly came to Miley's side as the crowd of fake Hannahs started pulling out their mobiles.

Oliver ran up. "Hey guys, I found her. She's on-stage!"

"Good work," Miley said sarcastically.

"Hold on, guys, I got a little something stuck in my craw," Luann said.

Miley watched, horrified, while Luann hawked up a loogie and spat it across the room and into the punch bowl. How many pictures of that would show up on the Internet tomorrow?

The whole crowed groaned in disgust.

"Bingo!" Luann laughed.

"She's gonna have a real hard time spitting with my fist in her mouth," Miley said between clenched teeth. She started towards the stage.

Lilly pulled her back. "You can't. If you get into something with her she may rip off your wig, too."

Oliver drew his plastic sword and stepped in front of them. "Have no fear, ladies, the masked musketeer has a plan."

Miley rolled her eyes and watched him disappear into the crowd. "Great. My life in the hands of Count Chesthair," she said, before following behind him.

Luann was still on-stage, getting ready to expose Miley's secret. "So, everybody, lookie here," she said into the microphone. "You're about to see something you never expected to see –" Luann reached for her wig, but before she could pull it off the lights went out.

When the lights came back on, the stage was empty. The audience was totally confused. A few people clapped half-heartedly and then Traci took the stage.

"Ooh, look at that. Magic. And spitting. Neat," she said, trying to save the party even though she thought her ex-friend Hannah must have totally lost her mind. "Why don't we have dessert now?" She called out to the waiters. "Bring out the Hannah Banana cream pie!

Backstage, Lilly was holding on to Luann so that she couldn't get away.

"You are so busted, Luann," Miley said.

"Guys, you grabbed the wrong one in the dark!" Luann said, using her Miley accent again. She struggled to get out of Lilly's tight grip. "I'm Miley!"

"Nice try, you backwoods witch," Miley snarled. "They're my best friends. They're not going to fall for that." She turned to Lilly and Oliver for support. "Tell her."

Lilly and Oliver looked from Miley to Luann and then at each other. Which girl was Miley and which was her cousin?

"You got any idea?" Oliver asked Lilly.

"Not a clue," Lilly admitted.

Oliver grabbed hold of Miley, just in case she was Luann.

"Please," Luann begged, still pretending to be Miley. "We have to get her out of here before she reveals my secret!"

"You mean *my* secret," Miley said.

"Wait a minute. I have an idea," Oliver said. "I know how to tell which one is the real Miley. Both of you kiss me."

"Okay," Luann said with a big smile, getting ready to pucker up.

"Ewwww," Miley said, her face twisting in disgust.

Oliver pointed to the girl who didn't want to kiss him. "That's Miley," he said.

Chapter Six

Once the real Miley was revealed, Oliver and Lilly were able to help their friend hustle Luann out to the limo. Hannah's reputation and Miley's secret identity were both safe. And the real Hannah Montana was able to go back to the party and do a little damage control with Traci.

Back at home, Miley told her father the whole story. Mr Stewart was visibly stunned by Luann's behaviour. He had to hand it to Miley. She had been right about Luann all along.

"And what has all this taught you?" Miley asked.

"That parents should believe their kids when they tell them their cousins are evil," he said, still wearing his scarecrow costume.

"And . . . ?" Miley asked leadingly.

"I should always take my mobile phone when I leave the house in case my daughter gets tied up in her wardrobe."

But that still wasn't enough for Miley. She wanted more. "And . . .?"

"I'm sorry," her father said, "but you don't have to worry about it much longer. Your uncle's on his way here to pick up Luann. They'll be gone tomorrow."

So soon? Miley hadn't even come up with a plan for revenge yet. "That doesn't give me much time to get her back," she said.

"Like I always told you, an eye for an eye makes the whole world blind," Mr Stewart said.

Miley might have taken his advice, if their neighbour hadn't run through the front door at that moment. Mr Dontzig's Mr Happy Pumpkin Man hat had fallen over one eye and there was dirt all over his face. His costume was in tatters. Stuffing fell around his feet as he slammed the door behind him.

"Stewart, you've got to help me," Mr Dontzig said, totally out of breath. "Those candy grabbers are like piranhas! And they're coming by the busload! It's like someone put an ad in the paper."

Mr Stewart smiled. "The paper?" he said. "That's way too slow. If someone wanted to get information out fast, they'd go down Pacific Coast Highway with a bullhorn."

Mr Dontzig gasped. "You didn't!"

Mr Stewart picked up a bullhorn. "Oh, yes, I did," he said into it, as he watched the truth dawn on his neighbour's face. "Gotcha!"

Mr Dontzig looked on in horror while Mr Stewart waved to the children who had followed Mr Happy Pumpkin Man to his house. "Okay, kids, come on down," he called to them. "Don't be shy."

"Curse you, Stewart!" Mr Dontzig yelled, running for the back door. "Curse you!"

The children cheered, ran through the front door, and then out the back again on the heels of the happy pumpkin man.

"Dad, what about revenge making the whole world blind?" Miley asked, watching cowboys, ballerinas, ghosts and princesses chase after her neighbour.

"I'm teaching that to you," her father said with a you-caught-me shrug. "It's too late for me."

The front door opened again and Jackson rode in on a pony. "Hey, Dad, Dontzig's pony followed me home. Can we keep him?" Jackson lowered his voice and spoke for the pony: "Please? All I need is a really big litter box."

Miley put on her best pouty expression. She wanted to keep the pony, too.

Jackson rode the pony towards the stairs. "I'm just gonna take him up to my room, okay?"

Mr Stewart didn't tell Jackson that horses don't walk up stairs. He'd have to find out the hard way.

* * *

The next morning, Mr Stewart was in the

"That is the best song you've ever written.
I can't wait to record it," Miley said.

"Uncle Robby, Daddy said that these were
your favourite Halloween cookies," said Luann.
"I made them myself."

"See how clever she is?" Miley asked Lilly.
"She tricked me into accusing her of something she
hadn't done so I'd look stupid."

"Yeah," Luann agreed. "Kinda like what we
used to do with Aunt Pearl's roadkill ravioli."

"Hey, the limo's here to take us to Traci's party. You ready?" Lilly asked.

"Maybe if you went to rodeo camp with the rest of us, you wouldn't be stuck in this sitchiation," said Luann.

"Yes!" Jackson said. "There is no way
Dontzig's house is scarier than ours."

"Guys, you grabbed the wrong one in the
dark!" Luann said. "I'm Miley!"

Part Two

"Honey, you're not actually meeting the queen until Sunday," Mr. Stewart said. "You look fine."

"Well, my, I should say you sure are livin' high on the hog. Quite a few hogs by the looks of it," Mam'aw replied.

"I got your message. Waxy aeroplane earphones?"
Lilly asked. "You're kidding, right?"

"But we're kinda caught between the queen
and a hard place, here," said Mr. Stewart.

"Robby Ray, ladies and gentlemen!" Miley announced. "You've been a beautiful audience, pip-pip, ta-ta, cheer-i-o, good night!"

"Jackson Stewart will now be playing with the woman who puts the 'Ruth' in 'ruthless'," announced Oliver.

"Oh, it's on. It's on," Mam'aw said.
"It's on like mud on a pig."

Your grandma's in the car alone, and sooner or
later she's gonna sniff out those pork scratchings I've
got hidden under the seat," said Mr. Stewart.

kitchen when the doorbell rang.

"Hey, Miley," he yelled upstairs. "Tell your cousin her daddy's here!"

Mr Stewart's brother, Bobby Ray, looked as much like Robby Ray as Luann looked like Miley. Only, like Luann, he wore Tennessee clothes – a giant cowboy hat and a blue shirt with white fringe.

Luann's father strutted into the room. "Put your drawers on Robby Ray, your brother's here."

"Good to see you, too, Bobby Ray," Mr Stewart said.

"Well, smack my goat and call me stupid. This sure is one humdinger of a shack ya got yourself," Bobby Ray drawled.

Mr Dontzig walked in right behind Luann's father. "Stewart! I need that pony back, it's a rental," he said. "Hey," he added, noticing Luann's father. Then he did a double take and screamed. "Ahhhh! Two Stewarts!"

Mr Dontzig dashed out of the house, grabbing leftover Halloween candy as he ran.

The Stewart brothers looked at each other with amused expressions.

"Hey, is he that pain-in-the-keister neighbour you been telling me about?" Bobby Ray asked.

Miley's father nodded. "Yep."

"Sure runs fast!" Luann's father said.

"He sure does," Mr Stewart agreed.

Together, the two brothers watched Mr Dontzig run. There was just one expression to describe their reaction and they used it at the same time:

"Eeeee, doggies!"

PART TWO

Chapter One

Miley nervously eyed the two empty, throne-like chairs in the hotel ballroom and checked her make-up.

"Honey, you're not actually meeting the queen until Sunday," her father said. "You look fine." He was wearing the disguise he always wore when he was acting as Hannah Montana's manager – a dark brown wig, long sideburns and a moustache.

"Yeah, you're right," Miley said, fluffing the long blonde hair on her Hannah wig. "But *you* don't," she said, laughing. She dabbed her father's nose with cover-up.

"Okay, darling," he joked. "That may work for the Backstreet Boys, but it's not quite my style."

Miley snapped her compact closed and slipped it into the pocket of her jeans.

Simon, the queen's butler, was telling the hotel staff where to place the huge baskets of flowers that had just been delivered. He stopped long enough to give Miley a lesson in royal manners.

"Now, Ms Montana," he said, "prior to your performance on Sunday for the queen's granddaughter, you will be introduced to her Royal Majesty."

Miley was superexcited about meeting the queen and her granddaughter. As Hannah

Montana, she had met lots of Hollywood celebrities, but no one as famous as the queen of England. She did a little conga dance while she sang. *"I'm gonna meet the queen, whoo! I'm gonna meet the queen, whoo!"*

Simon sniffed in disapproval. He didn't even crack a grin, but he did try to be funny. "Not if you do that, whoo!" he said, imitating her dance. Then he got serious. "Now, when cued, what you *will* do is the following. . . ."

Miley watched the butler's feet and tried to follow, bending her knees.

"Right foot behind left heel, knees bent, curtsy and say 'Hellooooo, Your Majesty,'" he said.

Miley spread her arms wide for balance and practised a small, wobbly curtsy. "Hellooooo, Your Majesty," she said, imitating Simon's accent.

"No, no, no," Simon said. "Lower."

"Hellooooo Your Majesty," Miley said again, lowering her voice.

Simon shook his head. "No, I meant, get lower."

Miley deepened her voice as much as she could. "Hellooooo, Your Majesty." She looked up with a big smile, but Simon still wasn't impressed.

"I'm talking about the curtsy," Simon said drily, shaking his head.

He was ready to give up on Miley completely and move on to teaching her father to bow, but Mr Stewart's mobile rang.

"Hello? Hey, Ma," Mr Stewart said. "Yeah, look we're right in the middle of rehearsing to meet the queen, can I –" He was silent for a moment, then Miley heard. "No, no, no, not Latifah."

Hannah Montana had met Queen

Latifah at a Hollywood movie premiere a few months before. "Hey, Simon," Miley said. "When I met *that* Queen, all I had to rehearse was . . ." Miley struck a pose, ". . . whassup, girlfriend?"

Simon simply stared.

Didn't this guy have a sense of humour? "Ya get it?" Miley asked, prodding him to crack a smile.

The smile didn't come. "Yes, unfortunately, I did," Simon said.

Mr Stewart was still on the phone and Miley's grandmother was clearly giving him a hard time. "Ma, I'm talking about the queen of England. Yeah, look, I'm kinda busy right now so can we . . ." Mr Stewart stopped speaking for a moment. "Yes, I know she didn't birth me."

"Mam'aw means well," Miley explained to Simon. "It's just when things don't go just the way she likes them, she can be . . . a royal pain."

Simon was about to respond when another servant entered the ballroom with an alarmed expression.

"The queen's granddaughter would like her pony groomed and brought to her room," she said.

Simon turned to Miley. Clearly he knew all about people who wanted things just the way they liked them. "Trust me, there's no royal pain like *the* royal pain." Then he turned back to the servant with as much dignity as he could muster. "Gwendolyn, I'll be needing a bucket of sudsies and my pony sponge."

Mr Stewart flipped his mobile phone closed just as Simon left the room. "He thinks he's got problems. Our mam'aw says she's flying in from Tennessee. She's in a cab on the way to the house right now."

Miley's brown eyes widened in surprise. Then she realized why her Dad looked so alarmed. "Dad, don't panic. We only left Jackson home alone for an hour. How much damage could he do?" Then she realized just how big of a mess her brother could make in a few minutes, let alone an hour.

Mr Stewart did, too. "We've got to move," he answered, running for the door.

By the time Miley and her father got back to the house, it looked like Jackson had been home alone for weeks. Sweatpants and a T-shirt were draped on the back of the sofa. A boogie board was propped against the piano, a volleyball sat in the chair and there were food containers everywhere.

Mr Stewart was filling a giant rubbish bag, naming the empty food containers as he threw them in. "Egg rolls, pizza, taquitos," he said. "I leave you at home alone for an hour and when I come back, this place has turned into the International House of Leftovers."

"Take it easy, Dad." Jackson pitched a container of fried rice into the rubbish bag. "It's just Mam'aw."

"Just Mam'aw!" his father said, totally frustrated. "You're talking about the woman that gave me life . . . and never lets me forget it. But this time I'm not giving her anything to complain about." He handed Jackson the full rubbish bag. "Get rid of this," he ordered.

"I'm on it," Jackson said. He lifted the cover of the grand piano and dropped the bag inside.

Miley ran down the stairs. She had been watching for her grandmother from her bedroom window. "Hey, hey, hello people! Mam'aw's cab just came up." She waved her arms excitedly. "It's Mam'aw time!"

"Fasten your seat belts," Mr Stewart said grimly.

They heard Mam'aw Ruthie before they saw her.

"Tip? You want a tip?" she asked her cabdriver. "If you are not gonna use deodorant, make sure your back windows roll down."

"Well, at least she's in a good mood," Mr Stewart said. "Now you all just sit here and act like you're two perfect little angels who always listen to their father."

Miley and Jackson sat on the sofa and gave him their best "are you crazy?" look.

"Just pretend," Mr Stewart said. He

grabbed Jackson's boogie board and threw it out onto the sun deck.

With a confused expression, Miley pulled out a long loaf of French bread from behind a cushion. "What is this doing here?" she asked.

"I lost the remote," Jackson explained. "I needed something to change channels with."

Miley whacked her brother with the bread. He tried to pull it out of her hands and they started to struggle.

"Hey, give me that," Mr Stewart said, reaching for the bread. "Cut it out."

"Cut it out," Miley yelled at Jackson.

The top half of the bread broke off in Mr Stewart's hands, but Miley and Jackson were still wrestling for the rest of it when Mam'aw walked thorough the door.

"Fighting over a loaf of bread?" she said,

wagging her finger. "Robby Ray Stewart, don't you feed these children?" she scolded.

Uh-oh, Miley thought, eyeing her brother.

Then Mam'aw's smile gave her away. "It's a good thing I have a bag full of hard candies."

"Mam'aw!" Miley said jumping to her feet.

She and Jackson raced to give her a hug.

"Hey, Mum," Mr Stewart said. "It's good to see you." He stepped forward for his own hug, but Mam'aw dropped her suitcase into his open arms instead.

"Oh, it's good to see you, too, sweetie pie," she answered. "Hey, by the way, you've got a loose step outside. If we weren't blood, I would sue ya." She gave him a playful slap on the cheek.

Mr Stewart shook his head with a smile. Same old Mam'aw, he thought.

Chapter Two

The first thing Mam'aw did was make a Tennessee feast for her grandchildren – fried chicken, biscuits and corn on the cob. She filled Jackson's and Miley's plates full.

Mr Stewart came in with the post. "What do you think, Ma?" he asked. "Your baby boy's got himself a beach house in Malibu."

"Well, my, I should say you sure are living high on the hog." She peered at his stomach and gave it a pat. "Quite a few hogs by the look of it," she teased.

"So, ah, how long you say you're staying?" Mr Stewart teased back and gave her a playful kiss on the cheek.

"Oh, now, don't you worry, sweetie," she answered. "I'm only here for the weekend. You can go back to taking food out of your children's mouths on Monday."

"Well, this is great, Mam'aw," Miley said excitedly. "Now you've got to come with us to meet the queen."

"Well, that sounds like fun, sweetie."

"Yeah, and I get to perform my new song for her, then I –"

Mam'aw cut off Miley to beam at Jackson. "But the real reason that I am here is because Jackson has made it to the finals of a big Los Angeles volleyball tournament."

Jackson pumped his fist in the air. "Oh, yeah," he said.

Miley smiled at him. Jackson was totally excited about this tournament. He had talked about nothing else for days.

"That reminds me," Mam'aw said to Jackson. "I have got something for you."

Jackson's face lit up. He stood to hug her again.

Mam'aw put her hands on her grandson's shoulders and looked into his eyes. "I have never been so proud of a grandchild in my whole life," she said, leading Jackson into the living room to give him his gift.

Miley's face fell as she watched them go. *Never* been so proud? she wondered. "Did I mention I was meeting the queen?" she asked meekly.

But they didn't hear her. They weren't even paying attention.

"Now, don't worry about it, baby doll," Mr Stewart said. "Mam'aw's gonna have time to do both. The queen's in the morning and the tournament's not till the afternoon."

But that wasn't it. Miley had hoped that this time things with Mam'aw would be different – that Mam'aw would pay attention to *her*, for once. But Mam'aw was just the same as ever. She acted like every little thing Jackson did or said was perfect, but she barely noticed Miley at all. "Daddy, she's doing it again," Miley said. "Every time she comes she treats Jackson like he's an angel and I'm invisible."

Mr Stewart checked to make sure his mother wasn't watching. He reached for a drumstick and took a big bite.

"Robby Ray, put that down," his mother called from the living room. "How big do you wanna get?"

Mr Stewart smiled at his daughter and put the chicken down with a sigh. "Trust me, honey. Sometimes being invisible has its advantages."

Miley smiled back, but she didn't agree. Mam'aw gave Daddy a hard time, but that was only because she loved him. And it was obvious she loved Jackson. Miley wouldn't mind a little of that love herself.

She got up and went over to see what Mam'aw had brought for Jackson.

"Now, way back in '64, when this old bag o' bones was on the Olympic volleyball team, I wore my lucky wristband." Mam'aw reached into her bag, pulled out a blue wristband and handed it to Jackson.

"Oh, this is so cool!" Jackson said, giving her a hug. "Thanks Mam'aw."

"Wow, that's so great of you to bring something special for Jackson," Miley said.

Her tone made it clear that she hoped there was something special in Mam'aw's bag for her, too.

"Oh, well, you don't think I forgot about you, now. Do you, sweetie?" Mam'aw asked.

Miley's face lit up at the thought of a present. But it quickly became clear that Mam'aw had forgotten her – at least until the last minute.

"Let me see what I have in here for you." Mam'aw rummaged through her bag. "Well, I know how much you love music, so I brought you aeroplane headphones!"

Was Mam'aw actually giving her used headphones from the aeroplane? "Wow, I don't know what to say." Miley forced herself to smile.

"You might wanna disinfect those," Mam'aw said. "I took 'em off the old guy who was sitting next to me. You can make a candle with the earwax on those things."

Miley tried to keep the disappointment from showing on her face and to look on the bright side of the situation. "Two for one," she said, scraping the disgusting old-guy earwax off the headphones.

The next morning, Jackson and Mam'aw played a dance game on electronic mats in front of the television. Miley ran downstairs to join them, but she saw right away that there was only room for two players – just the way Mam'aw and Jackson wanted it. She went outside and sat on the deck by herself, watching Jackson and Mam'aw have a good time without her.

"C'mon, you gotta do better than that if you're gonna be a volleyball champion," Mam'aw urged.

Jackson huffed and puffed, trying to keep up with her.

"Your mam'aw can do better!" she said. "Heck your mam'aw *is* doing better than that."

Jackson sped up, but he got the dance moves all wrong and tripped over his own feet. "Ow! Ow!" he moaned. "Cramp in the leg. Cramp in the leg. I'm going down." He fell to his knees and then rolled onto his back, clutching his thigh.

"Jackson, c'mon, now. Get up, baby," Mam'aw said. "If I stop now at my age, I'm gonna lock up like a Yarn Barn at nine o'clock. I'll stretch you out." She grabbed Jackson's leg and stretched.

"Owwww!" Jackson moaned.

"Embrace the pain," she coached, stretching his leg again.

Jackson groaned.

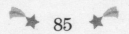

"Yeah. You're gonna thank me for this later," Mam'aw promised.

Lilly ran up the stairs to the deck and dropped onto a bench next to Miley. "Hey, Miley, I got your message. Waxy aeroplane earphones?" she asked. "You're kidding, right?"

Miley held up the earphones. "With little grey hairs still stuck to them," she said glumly.

"Ewwww!" Lilly said, trying not to gag.

"I don't understand, Lilly," Miley said, dropping the earphones. "I'm always nice to her. And I even complimented her on her orthopedic shoes." She shook her head sadly. Mam'aw hadn't even said thank you. She just turned to Jackson and asked him to recount his last volleyball game, for, like, the millionth time. "Trust me, Lilly, those were *frankenboots*."

"Listen, Miley," Lilly said. "I know you think she might like Jackson better, but that can't be true."

"It is," Miley insisted. "It's like I don't exist and she has him up on a pedestal."

Lilly thought her friend had to be exaggerating. "Oh, come on," she said.

"No, you come on," Miley said, leading Lilly to the door.

They looked into the living room. Jackson was standing on a kitchen chair – as if he were up on a pedestal – while Mam'aw massaged his calves.

"That's my little champion," Mam'aw said.

Jackson's eyes were closed. He had a blissful smile on his face. Clearly, he was totally loving the massage *and* the attention.

Her little champion? Even Lilly had to admit that was a bit extreme.

"I don't even think she wants to come watch me perform for the queen," Miley said as she walked back over to the bench and sat down in a slump.

Lilly smiled. She had been dying to meet the queen. "I have an idea! And it's so simple you're going to love it."

"What?" Miley asked.

"Dump Granny and take me," Lilly said.

But Miley was determined to take Mam'aw. Maybe if her grandmother saw how popular and loved Hannah Montana was, she'd pay more attention to Miley. "No. She's going. She's going if I have to tie her up like a deer and strap her to the bonnet of my daddy's car."

Chapter Three

Jackson and his volleyball partner, Topher, practised in the school gym while Mam'aw looked on from the bleachers ready to jump in with pointers.

Oliver, the tournament's announcer, sat at a table with the sound equipment, practising his own moves. "Topher sets for Jackson," Oliver said into the microphone. "Jackson leaps and . . ." Oliver paused to watch the action. "Right into the net!" He hit a button that filled the gym with the sound of a cartoon character dying.

Jackson glared at him.

"What?" Oliver asked innocently. "If I'm going to announce the tournament, I need to practise, too."

"If you're going to announce for the tournament, you're going to need to be alive," Jackson warned.

Oliver pretended to be scared and combined it with the sound effect of a crowd shouting, "Oooo."

Jackson glared at him again and then went back to practise.

"Jackson takes the set from Topher and …" Oliver announced in a dramatic whisper.

Jackson jumped to spike the ball, but somehow he caught it and then dropped it instead of hitting it over the net.

Oliver didn't say a word. He didn't have

to. He hit a button and the gym was filled with the sound of a bomb dropping.

Jackson didn't need the sound effect to know that he was totally bombing. And the fact that he was bombing in front of Mam'aw made things even worse. His face burned with embarrassment.

Mam'aw Ruthie realized she needed to take control of this disaster before things got even worse. Oliver was first on her list. She walked over to the announcer's table. "Oliver, do you have the sound of a truck running over a microphone?" she asked, putting her arm around him.

Oliver checked his machine. "Nope, I don't have that one."

"You will if you push another button," she warned.

Oliver raised his arms in surrender. No more sound effects.

With Oliver taken care of, Mam'aw knew it was time to get Jackson into the game. "You, kiddo, are doing great," she said, walking over to him. "You just need a little more knee bend."

Topher was next on her list. "And you, sweetheart," she said, grabbing him by the front of his T-shirt. "You either get your head into this game or I'm gonna have a senior moment all over your keister."

Jackson bounced the ball uneasily. He wasn't doing great, as Mam'aw had said. He knew it and Mam'aw knew it. "I'm sorry for screwing up," he told his grandmother. "I guess I'm just a little nervous."

"Well, you're supposed to be," she answered. "But you are a Stewart and Stewarts do not lose. Now, you want this, don't you?"

"I do!" Jackson said.

"Of course you do. So, stop your moping."

Oliver pushed another button. This time, it played the sound of a baby crying.

Mam'aw and Jackson both turned to him, looking totally annoyed.

"Finger slipped," Oliver said, raising his hands in the air again. "My bad."

Mam'aw picked up the volleyball and moved towards the net. "Now, I'm gonna set for ya. Okay, bend those knees."

Jackson crouched in position, bouncing up and down a little.

Mam'aw set the ball and Jackson let out a yell, giving a strong, firm hit – right in Oliver's direction. Oliver had to move fast to get out of the way. Now the gym was filled with the sound of his chair falling over as he fell to the floor and out of sight.

"Yeah!" Mam'aw said, raising her hands

for a high five. "That's what I'm talking about!"

The next day, Mr Stewart played his guitar while Miley finished rehearsing the final chorus of her song in the hotel ballroom. She wore white evening gloves and a pretty dress in honour of the queen. Of course, she had on her blonde Hannah wig, too.

"That was great, honey," Mr Stewart said.

Mam'aw barely heard the song. She paced impatiently while Jackson, wearing a suit and tie, tried to stretch his muscles.

"For heaven's sake," Mam'aw said, checking her watch. "That woman is over three hours late. Who does she think she is? The queen of England?"

Mr Stewart just stared at her.

"Well, it's still no excuse," Mam'aw said.

"She's right," Jackson added. I've got the biggest match of my life in an hour. I shouldn't even be here."

His father tried to calm them both down. "Don't worry, son, it's all going to work out."

"When?" Jackson asked, totally frustrated. "I'm starting to tighten up."

Mam'aw Ruthie shook her head. Tight players did not win volleyball tournaments. "Not good. You want me to stretch you out again?"

"No, no, no!" Jackson said, jumping out of her reach. Mam'aw's "gentle" stretches usually meant pain.

Simon, the queen's butler, came in. He had a bored expression on his face. "Excuse me, but the queen has been delayed at the state fair, where her granddaughter washed down chilli cheese fries with a grape slushy, producing a royal and colourful upchuck."

"Just hose her off and get her over here!" Mam'aw cried.

Simon sniffed. He clearly wasn't used to hearing the queen and her granddaughter talked about that way.

Mr Stewart tried to save the situation. "I think what my mum's trying to say is we have another commitment, so –"

"Oh, not a problem," Simon answered, cutting him off. "I'll just tell the queen you stood her up for a monster-truck jamboree."

Mr Stewart raised an eyebrow. He knew an insult when he heard it. "You think if there was a monster-truck jamboree any-where within spittin' distance of this place we'd be here?" he drawled with a straight face.

"Daddy!" Miley said. Was her family going to ruin her meeting with the queen?

"I guess we'll just wait," Mr Stewart said.

"Duh," Simon answered rudely before leaving the room again.

"Well, this is crazy. We can't wait," Mam'aw said. She started after Simon. "Yo, Hamlet! You get your queen on the horn a-sap," she yelled.

"Get back here, Ma!" Mr Stewart ran after his mother, then stopped and cringed when he saw what she was up to. "You cannot give a grown man a wedgie."

Miley watched her father leave and then turned to her brother. "She's going to insult the queen and ruin my command performance all because of her 'little Jackson.' It's always about you," Miley complained.

"Me?" Jackson asked in disbelief. "It's never about me! Everything in this family revolves around you."

"What are you talking about?" Miley asked.

"If it's not the queen, it's a concert. If it's not a concert, it's a CD signing," he said. "I mean, face it, no matter how important something is to me, it always comes in second to Hannah Montana."

Miley rolled her eyes. "Come on, Jackson. You know that's not true."

"Yes, it is," Jackson answered, heading for the door.

"Where are you going?" Miley asked.

"To *my* volleyball match. Something that's important to me. Tell the queen I said *hellooooo*," he said, while imitating a curtsy.

With a concerned expression, Miley watched him storm off. Was Jackson right? she wondered.

Chapter Four

Miley sat in a chair staring into space. She was still thinking about what Jackson had said when Mam'aw and Mr Stewart came back into the ballroom.

"Oh, for heaven's sake, Robby Ray," Mam'aw said. "I wasn't going to hit him. I just wanted to give him a little Tennessee talkin' to."

"Yeah, last time you gave someone a

little Tennessee talkin' to, the air marshal made him land the plane!"

"Ask for an extra bag of peanuts and all of a sudden you are a threat to national security," she said, shaking her head. Then she noticed that Jackson was missing. "Where's Jackson?" she asked Miley.

"He left for his volleyball tournament," Miley said with a frown. "So I suppose you want to go now, too."

"Well, if I don't, who will?" Mam'aw asked. "I don't see either of you heading for the door."

Miley and Mr Stewart followed her.

"Ma, you don't think we want to be there for him?" Mr Stewart asked. "Of course, we do. But we're kinda caught between the queen and a hard place here."

Miley nodded in agreement. What were they supposed to do, walk out on the queen?

"And so, once again, Jackson gets the short end of the stick," Mam'aw said.

Mr Stewart shook his head. "Mum, that's not fair."

"It is too fair!" Mam'aw said. "Now, I know you both love him, but you're so busy taking care of Hannah Montana you're letting poor Jackson Stewart fall through the cracks."

Miley's face fell. She knew how that felt. That was exactly what her grandmother was doing to her. "Mam'aw, you're so busy with Jackson that you're letting me fall through the cracks," she said, blinking back tears.

"Oh, Miley, sweetie," her grandmother said.

"Just forget it," Miley said. She turned her back on her grandmother and headed back into the ballroom.

Mr Stewart started after his daughter, but his mother stopped him.

"No, hold up," she said. "I need to do this." She found Miley in the ballroom and sat down next to her. "Miley, sweetie. I am sorry if I made you think that I don't care. But the truth is, I love you very much and I am so proud of everything you do."

"Really?" Miley asked, confused. "You've never said that to me before."

Mam'aw smiled at her. "Well, I guess I was so busy making sure that Jackson got some attention, that I didn't have enough left for you."

"Mam'aw, do you know how that makes me feel?"

"Kind of invisible?" Mam'aw asked.

"Yeah," Miley nodded.

"Maybe that's the way your brother feels all the time."

"Really?" Miley had to think about that for a minute. "He never said anything."

Mam'aw ran her hand down Miley's check with a smile and gently pushed a strand of Miley's long blonde wig away from her face. "What's he gonna say, sweetie? Don't be Hannah Montana? He wouldn't be a very good brother if he said that, now, would he?"

"No, I guess not," Miley said with a sigh. "And I guess I wouldn't be a very good sister if I made you stay here." She smiled. She still wished Mam'aw could stay and watch her perform for the queen, but it was more important for Jackson to have someone cheering him on at the volleyball tournament. "Go, we'll catch up with you later."

"I love you, kiddo," Mam'aw said, giving Miley a big hug. "You rock that queen's world. I cannot wait to hear all about it."

"Thanks, Ma," Mr Stewart said. He gave his mother a hug as she left the room. "It's nice to see the soft side of you once in a while."

But Mam'aw's soft side was already gone. "I appreciate that, baby boy," she said, patting his stomach. "And you stay away from that dessert table or all of your sides are gonna be soft."

Mr Stewart shook his head with a grin and watched her leave. "I was a chubby child," he told Miley. "She could never let that go."

Miley's mind was on Jackson, not on her father's "soft side." "I feel awful, Daddy," she said. "We're going to miss Jackson all because of me."

"It's not your fault. There's nothing you can do unless you know some way to speed up time."

Speed up time? Well maybe . . . Miley thought, as she started to form a plan.

By the time the queen finally arrived, an hour later, Miley had clued her father in to her plan.

Hannah Montana and her manager stood in front of the stage listening to a classical string trio play a slow piece. The ballroom was full of people waiting to meet the queen and hear Hannah Montana's concert.

The ballroom doors opened.

"Ladies and gentlemen, the queen," Simon announced with a flourish.

The trio started to play a slow march. The queen and her granddaughter walked down the aisle as if they had three days to get to their seats. It seemed to Miley that five minutes passed between each step.

"Sweet mercy, that woman makes a snail

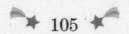

look like a cheetah," Mr Stewart whispered. "You ready, darling?"

"Let's kick it up, Daddy," Miley answered.

"Excuse me, partner," Mr Stewart said to one of the violinists. "I'll take it from here."

Simon spotted Mr Stewart taking the violin. A look of panic crossed his face, but he was too far away to do anything about it. "Oh, this can't be good," he muttered to himself.

Mr Stewart played the violin like the fiddle, launching into a square dance tune and shouting, "Yeehah!"

Miley clapped her hands and stomped her feet as if she were at a Tennessee hoedown, chanting along with the music and leading the queen and her granddaughter down the aisle. *Look at your guests, give 'em a* smile, get the lead out, move down the aisle!"

The queen looked totally confused, but her granddaughter beamed at Hannah Montana.

Miley spun the two of them around. *"Now, swing that girl, give her a push, there's your seat, now plant that tush!"* Then she spun them again, this time right into their seats.

The crowd looked on, amazed – no one had ever treated the queen that way before. But Miley simply raised her arms in the air and announced, "The queen, ladies and gentlemen," before dancing over to the stage.

"Okay, hit it Robby Ray!"

Mr Stewart grabbed his guitar and started to play.

Miley launched into her song, singing at triple speed while her father raced to keep up with her on his guitar.

Still completely confused, the queen looked at her granddaughter. But the little girl was totally happy to listen to Hannah Montana sing in person – even at triple speed.

Miley kept singing as fast as she possibly could. Then she threw things over to her father. "Guitar solo!" she shouted, pointing at him.

Mr Stewart played one note on the guitar.

"Robby Ray, ladies and gentlemen," Miley announced. "You've been a beautiful audience, pip-pip, ta-ta, cheer-i-o, good night!" She grabbed her father's arm and raced for the door.

The queen watched them leave and then turned to her butler. "Simon, have we just been punked?" she asked.

Chapter Five

Mam'aw arrived at the gym just in time. The bleachers were packed for the volleyball tournament and the games were about to start.

"There is my future champion," Mam'aw said, spotting Jackson. Then she noticed that instead of stretching out and getting ready to win, Jackson was packing up his gear. "What are you doing?" she asked.

Jackson frowned. "I have to forfeit," he said.

"What?"

"Topher called, he's got the flu."

"Well, that's no excuse," Mam'aw said. She had never forfeited anything in her life and she didn't think Jackson should, either. "Heck, during the Olympic qualifiers I got food poisoning. I blew chunks all over the court. The other team was sliding all over the place. We won in a landslide."

"Forget it, Mam'aw. He's not coming." Jackson was so totally bummed he couldn't even laugh at the idea of Mam'aw blowing chunks on the court. "Can you believe it? I think I could have won this thing and now I don't even get the chance to try." He headed out of the gym, convinced that his moment to shine was lost.

Mam'aw put her hands on his shoulders

and turned him around. "Oh, yes, you do, young man," she said. "I did not fly all the way out here from Tennessee just to watch you throw in the towel."

Mam'aw clearly didn't get the fact that the tournament was for two-man teams. He wasn't throwing in the towel because he wanted to. He didn't have a choice. "But I don't have a partner," Jackson explained.

"You mean you *didn't* have a partner," Mam'aw said.

Jackson looked at her. "Oh, no," he said.

"Oh, yes," Mam'aw answered with a big smile.

Jackson was alone on his side of the net when Oliver took his seat at the announcer's table. Lilly was next to him.

"Ladies and gentlemen, we have a last-minute substitution," Oliver said. "Jackson

Stewart will now be playing with the woman who puts the 'Ruth' in ruthless." He stopped to hit a button on his sound machine, filling the gym with the sound of an organ playing "Charge!"

"Slammin' Mam'aw Stewart!" Oliver announced.

Mam'aw ran into the gym wearing her Olympic volleyball uniform. She did a few quick star jumps, a couple of stretches and then gave Jackson a high five.

The other team cracked up when they saw her and realized they were going to be playing against an actual grandmother.

"You're kidding, right?" asked one of the opposing players.

Mam'aw walked up to the net. "Well, I just didn't want my grandson to have to forfeit," she said sweetly. "So I would appreciate it if y'all would go easy on us."

"Sure," the guy shrugged. "No problem."

Mam'aw turned around and winked at her grandson.

Oliver announced each move. "Jackson serves the ball. It's returned over the net," he said dramatically. "Jackson sets to Ruth and she spikes it home!"

"Ahhh! Ooooo-yaaa!" Mam'aw yelled when the ball hit the floor before the other team could get to it.

She and Jackson gave each other a high five.

"Hey! What was that?" asked the player who had agreed to go easy on them.

"Well, I didn't say *we* were going easy on *you*, Slick!" Mam'aw laughed.

"All right!" the player answered, rising to the challenge. "Bring it on, grandma!"

"Oh, it's on," Mam'aw said. "It's on. It's on like mud on a pig."

It was a close match. Oliver could hardly keep up, but the crowd was cheering so loudly that they wouldn't have been able to hear his announcements anyway.

Lilly watched Mam'aw fall to her knees to return a serve. Jackson set Mam'aw up for a spike and the other team missed the ball. Then Mam'aw set him up and Jackson scored a point.

They were on the verge of winning when Miley and Mr Stewart ran into the gym.

"We made it," Mr Stewart said. "Come on, there's some seats." He headed for the bleachers.

Miley crouched behind Lilly and Oliver to get an update on the game. "Hey, y'all. What's the score?"

Lilly didn't take her eyes off the court. "If Jackson scores the next point, they win." Then she turned to look at Miley and gasped. "Omigosh, you're Hannah Montana!" she squealed.

Oliver put his hand over the microphone. Luckily, everyone was too into the game to hear what Lilly said.

Miley didn't understand what the big deal was all of a sudden. "Lilly, you've known this for months. Helloooo! Get over it," she said.

"No, I mean you're Hannah Montana, now!" Lilly told her. If the kids in the gym realized that Hannah was in their midst, it would cause a stampede. She grabbed both sides of Miley's long, blonde Hannah wig and held them in front of her friend's face.

Miley looked at her hair, cross-eyed. She was in such a hurry to get to Jackson's game that she had totally forgotten to take off her Hannah Montana disguise. "Oh, no! This is supposed to be Jackson's big

moment. Hannah Montana can't spoil it."
Miley ducked under the announcer's desk.

"Start crawling," Lilly said. "We'll get you to the stands."

Slowly, she and Oliver moved the desk across the floor while Miley crawled underneath.

Oliver kept announcing the game, trying to watch it and also keep up with the moving microphone. "This is it. Jackson Stewart serving for the gold," he said dramatically. "This is, without a doubt, the most important serve of young Stewart's life."

The table stopped and Miley darted behind the bleachers.

"If he blows this –" Oliver said. He was getting carried away with the drama.

Suddenly, Oliver's microphone shut off. He hit it a couple of times, but it had gone dead. Mam'aw had marched over and unplugged it from the sound machine.

"Son, you sound a whole lot better when no one can hear you," she said, leaning over him.

She turned to Jackson and saw the nervous expression on his face. Mam'aw put her hands on his shoulders. "Relax, the crowd is here for you. Everybody is here for *you*," she said.

"Not everyone," Jackson said.

"Look again," Mam'aw told him.

Jackson looked into the bleachers and saw his dad. Miley spread her father's calves apart and waved to her brother from underneath the bleachers.

Jackson smiled. Suddenly, he wasn't so nervous anymore. He took a deep breath and served the ball. The other team hit it back. Jackson had to dive to save it, but he managed to hit it over the net. Mam'aw saw the other team volley the ball. It was high in the air. She got down on her hands and knees. Jackson hopped onto her back and did a 360-degree turn in midair to spike the ball.

Jackson and Mam'aw won the game!

Mam'aw jumped to her feet and they gave each other high fives.

"Yes!" Jackson shouted, pumping his arm in the air. He was the winner of the volleyball tournament!

Mr Stewart whooped and hollered from the stands. Miley was so excited for Jackson that she forgot she was hiding under the bleachers. She jumped up and down for her brother. "Way to go, Jackson!" she yelled, hitting her head on the bleacher seat above her. "Ow!" she yelled.

A guy in the crowd heard the noise and turned around. "Hey, look!" he yelled. "It's Hannah Montana!"

The crowd suddenly went silent as all eyes turned to Miley.

Miley grabbed her father's calves and closed them in front of her face. "No, it's not!" she said.

"She's under the stands!" yelled a girl.

"No, I'm not," Miley said again.

But it was too late. The crowd had seen her.

Miley darted out from behind the bleachers and ran for the door, her high heels in her hand. The crowd raced after her, screaming for autographs. In seconds, the bleachers were empty.

"Way to go, son," Mr Stewart said, shaking Jackson's hand and giving him a pat on the back. But he was running after the crowd at the same time. "I better go check on your sister," he said.

Jackson watched his father leave and picked up his trophy from the announcer's desk. "Amazing," he said to Mam'aw. "Even when I win, it's still all about Hannah Montana."

"No it's not. This is all about you, sweetie," Mam'aw said, taking him by the shoulders. "You won. And nobody can take that away from you." She eyed the statue in Jackson's hands. "Now give me my trophy," she said, snatching it away.

Jackson looked on, amazed. Was she really taking his trophy?

"I'm just kidding," Mam'aw said, laughing at her own joke. She gave the trophy back and pulled Jackson into a hug.

Miley had finally managed to evade the

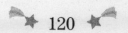

crowd and had borrowed Lilly's hoodie to hide her hair. She and her father went back to the gym and found Jackson alone, sitting on the bleachers with his trophy.

Mr Stewart pulled off the moustache that was part of his disguise when he acted as Hannah Montana's manager. "Jackson, I have something I want to say to you, and when I do, I don't want this caterpillar on my lip." He patted Jackson's shoulder. "I'm proud of you, son."

"Thanks," Jackson said.

Mr Stewart knew Miley had something she wanted to say to her brother, too. "Well, why don't I give you two some time," Mr Stewart said. "Besides, your grandma's in the car alone and sooner or later she's gonna sniff out those pork scratchings I got hidden under the seat."

Miley watched him leave and then sat

down next to her brother. "Congratulations," she said.

"Thanks."

"Look, I'm sorry," Miley said. "I didn't mean to mess this up for you. It seems Hannah Montana does that a lot."

Jackson shrugged. "It's okay."

"No, it's not. I wouldn't blame you if you hated me."

"I don't hate you, Miles," Jackson said.

Miley raised her eyebrows. That's not what he said when she ate the last piece of chocolate cake last week or when she took too long in the bathroom yesterday.

"Okay, sure I'd like a little more attention sometimes," Jackson admitted. "But at the end of the day, I like who I am and that's all that really counts."

"So you're not mad about today?" Miley asked.

Jackson shook his head. "My sister and my dad blew off the queen of England just to watch me play volleyball. How could I be mad at that?" He was still kind of amazed that they had done it.

Miley leaned her head on her brother's shoulder and put her arm around him. Jackson rested his head on top of hers.

"I think this is the nicest moment we've ever had," Miley said.

"I know," Jackson said. "And if you tell anybody about it, I'll deny it."

"What conversation?" Miley asked with a smile.

"That's my little sis," he said.

Miley gave him a playful punch on the shoulder.

Just then Mam'aw ran across the gym carrying a bag of pork scratchings. "Comin' through!" she yelled.

Mr Stewart was on her heels, huffing and puffing. "Gimme back my pork scratchings, Ma!"

Mam'aw stopped and waved the bag under his nose. "If you'd quit eatin' all this fried garbage, maybe you could catch me!" she yelled, taking off again.

Miley and Jackson both cracked up as they watched Mr Stewart run after their grandmother.

Put your hands together for the next Hannah Montana book . . .

Seeing Green

Adapted by M.C. King

Based on the series created by Michael Poryes and Rich Correll & Barry O'Brien

Based on the episode, "More Than a Zombie To Me," Written by Steven Peterman

Miley loved her best friend Lilly, but sometimes the girl could be indecisive — unbelievably indecisive.

They'd been standing at the mirrors in the girls' toilets for practically all of their free period while Lilly played with her hair, unable to find a style that worked. Miley felt for Lilly, she *really* did. Everyone has had a bad hair day, after all. Still, Miley could think of so many better ways to spend their time – not to mention, more pleasant places to spend it in. . . .

Miley couldn't take it anymore. She was haired out. Plus, she had news – huge news! She needed to get Lilly's attention. "Uuhhghh . . ." she moaned, making a crazy face into the mirror. . . . Miley checked to make sure the coast was clear, then lowered her voice just in case. "Guess which famous pop star is going to play Zaronda, Princess of the Undead, on 'Zombie High?'"